Story by
Christa Galer

Illustrations & Layout by
Jeffrey Galer

ISBN 0-9706491-0-X

Printed in the United States of America

For Kayleigh, Megan and You.

My name is Charles, but you can call me Chip. I live on the edge of a stream near a farm. I want to tell you about my adventure. It's about how I met my new friends.

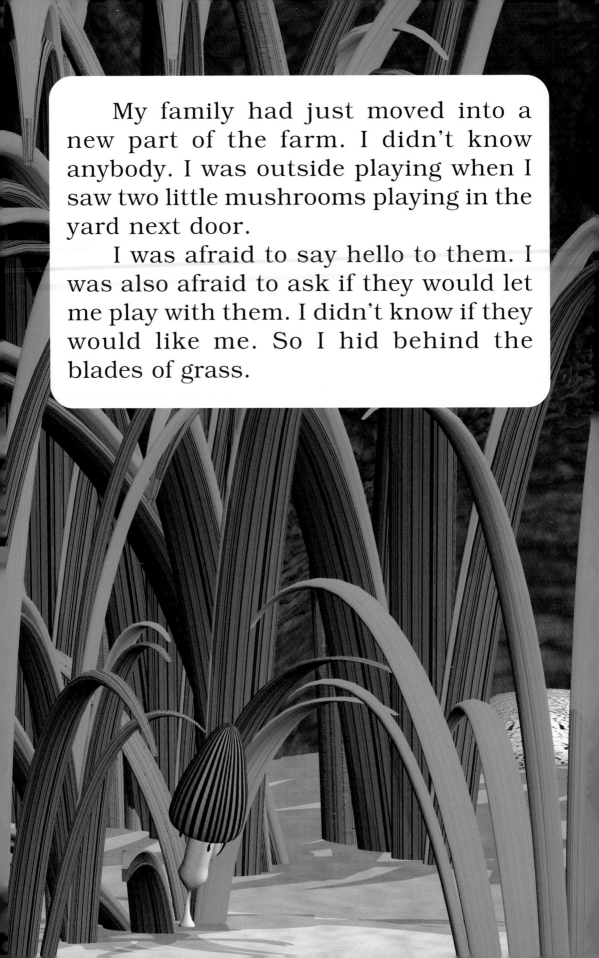

My family had just moved into a new part of the farm. I didn't know anybody. I was outside playing when I saw two little mushrooms playing in the yard next door.

I was afraid to say hello to them. I was also afraid to ask if they would let me play with them. I didn't know if they would like me. So I hid behind the blades of grass.

I watched them having lots of fun. I heard the mushroom boy say, "Hope, I want to go on an adventure."

Hope said, "What kind of adventure Edger?"

"I want to go to the Big Red Barn." Said Edger.

Hope wasn't sure, but she wanted to be like her big brother so she hopped beside Edger through the farm. I followed them.

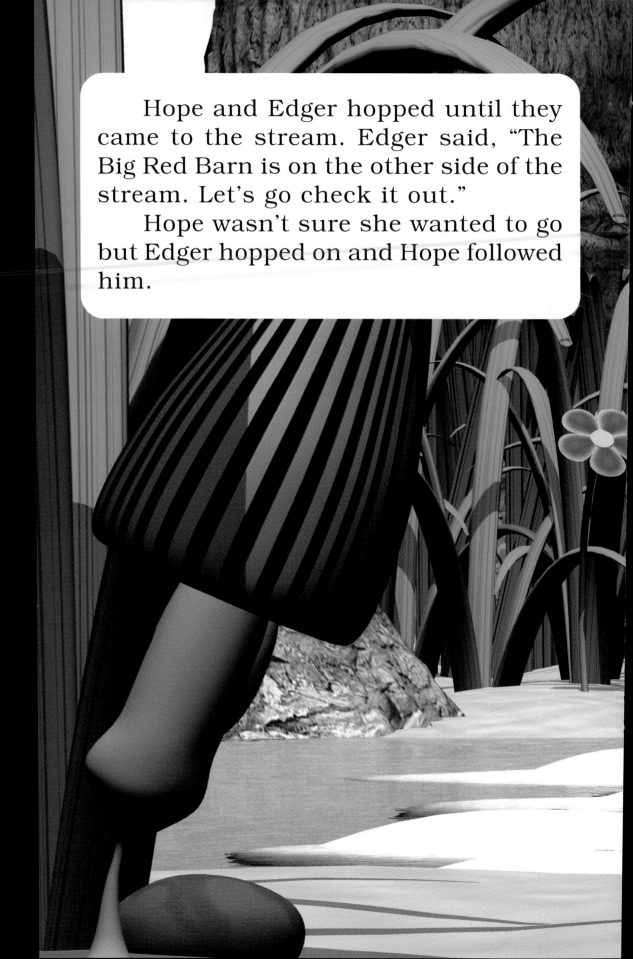

Hope and Edger hopped until they came to the stream. Edger said, "The Big Red Barn is on the other side of the stream. Let's go check it out."

Hope wasn't sure she wanted to go but Edger hopped on and Hope followed him.

They hopped across the stream and up the bank. Suddenly over the top of the grass, I saw a giant building. It was the Big Red Barn. It was the biggest thing I had ever seen.

Edger and Hope hopped up and went inside the barn. I was afraid to go inside, but I didn't want to stay outside by myself so I followed them.

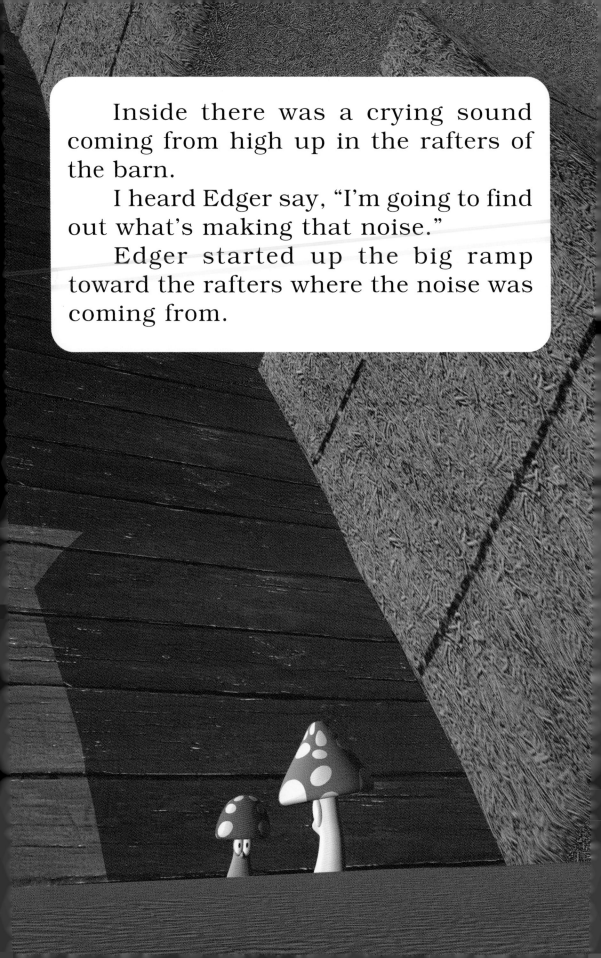

Inside there was a crying sound coming from high up in the rafters of the barn.

I heard Edger say, "I'm going to find out what's making that noise."

Edger started up the big ramp toward the rafters where the noise was coming from.

Hope followed her brother up the ramp to the rafters. I hid behind the bales of hay but I never let them out of my sight.

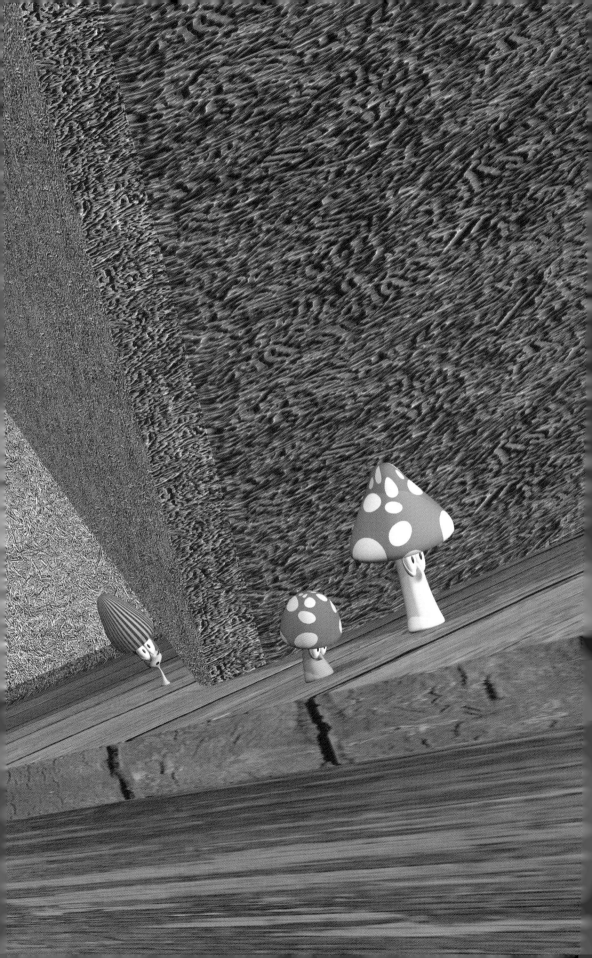

At the top of the ramp, high in the rafters, there was a caterpillar who was caught in a huge spider web. He was crying. Edger and Hope started to hop over to help him.

Just then I saw a big scary spider creeping down the wall. It was going toward the spider web on the ledge. I didn't know what to do !

It was heading for Edger and Hope. I was afraid the spider would hurt them. I had to do something! A rope was dangling from the ceiling. I grabbed the rope and swung across the barn and knocked the spider off the ledge.

"My name is Chip. We just moved into the tree next door to you. I saw you playing in your yard and was afraid you wouldn't want to be my friends. So I just followed you here."

"You followed us here? You should have asked to come along." said Hope. "We would love to be friends with you." said Edger.

All three of us pulled the caterpillar out of the web.

Hope said, "Hey, we can call him Slink. He can be our pet."

We all started home together. "Wow" said Chip, "This has been an exciting day. I made new friends and had a grand adventure. Next time I'll ask if I can play."

"That is a good idea." Said Edger. From that day on we have been friends.

The first of
many adventures.